KB176312

엘리트 시선 42

갠지스강 블루스

장 현 경 시집

엘리트출판사

갠지스강 블루스

장 현 경 시집

엘리트출판사

— 서문(序文)

여행 이야기

하지가 지나면 곧 소서(小暑)가 온다. 장마와 무더위가 기승을 부리는 여름을 그려본다. 좋은 글을 쓰려면 많이 읽고 쓰고 생각해야 한다. 다시 말해 글쓰기도 일종의 '기술'이 아닌가 한다. 좋은 글을 쓰기 위해서는 생각이 분명해야 한다. 이어 표현이 논리적이어야 한다. 따라서 체계화된 글의 내용이 어휘 선택, 문장의 구성 성분 등을 통하여 어떻게 적용되는지를 살펴볼 필요가 있다.

시는 곧 삶이다. 시는 영혼의 식량이요, 시대를 비추는 거울이다. 이런 관점에서 시인에게 필요한 것은 진실한 언행과 아름다운 삶이다. 즉 진실한 언행도 글을 잘 쓰자는 이야기이고 아름다운 삶도 글을 재미있게 쓰자는 말이다. 결국 그 많은 작가가 긴 세월을 갈고 닦아 자신을 최고의 명품으로 만들고 있다. 러시아의 대문호, 도스토옙스키처럼 5분을 헛되이 하지 않겠다는 마음을 되새기며, 우리 자신이 끊임없는 도전으로 무엇인가를 이루겠다는 결심을 스스로 해야 하겠다.

여행을 다니며 천혜의 자연을 만끽해 본다. 시인으로 움츠린 몸에 기지개를 켜며 사계절 다니는 여행 이야기를 소재로 여기 한 권의 영역 시집을 다듬는다. 여행 이야기가 이 어려운 시대를 견뎌내는 수많은 독자에게 위로와 희망, 감동이 되기를 기대합니다.

늘 따뜻한 성원을 보내주신 가족과 이웃의 지지에 고마운 마음 전하며 청계문학 가족 여러분의 건승을 빕니다. 나의 시편들을 만나는 존경하는 독자님께 건강과 행복이 늘 함께하시기를 기원합니다.

2021년 5월 청계서재(淸溪書齋)에서

자정(紫井) 장현경(張鉉景) 삼가 씀

- Preface

Travel Story

After the summer solstice, Shortly a Soseo(around July 7 on the solar calendar) will be coming. I imagine a summer when the rainy season and the heat are rampant. To write good writing, you need to read, write and think a lot. In other words, writing is a kind of 'skill'. To write a good article, you need to have a clear mind. Then, expression should be logical. Therefore, it is necessary to examine how the contents of a structured text are applied through vocabulary selection and sentence composition.

Poetry is life. Poetry is a provisions of soul, a mirror that reflects the times. In this respect, what a poet needs is true words and actions and beautiful lives. In other words, true words and actions are a story to write well, and beautiful life is about having fun writing well. In the end, many writers are polishing their long years to make themselves the best luxury goods. Like Dostoevsky, a great writer in Russia, we have to make up our minds to do something by ourselves, reminding ourselves not to waste 5 minutes with constant challenges.

I travel and enjoy the nature of heaven's blessing. I stretch my body as a poet and refine a book of poems translated into English here with the story of traveling for four seasons. It is hoped that the travel story will provide comfort, hope, and impression for many readers who endure this difficult age.

I am grateful to the support of my family and neighbors who have always been warmly supported and I wish you all the best in the Cheonggye literature family. I wish you all the health and happiness to the respectful readers who meets my poems.

May 2021 in Cheonggye Library
Jajeong Jang Hyun-kyung Raising

- 서시(序詩)

뭄타즈 마할

지상에서
가장 아름다운 사랑의 궁전
타지마할은
숨 막히게 조화롭고
보석처럼 눈부시다

오, 왕비여!
그대의 예쁜 마음씨에
맑은 목소리와 넘치는 애교
꾸밈없는 성품과 돋보인 지성이
몹시 그리운 어느 날

야무나강을 따라
아그라 성에서 타지마할로
그대를 찾으러
그대와 함께하려
길을 나서리

슬픔을 말하는 듯
타지마할에 누워 있는
그녀의 눈빛이
아무 말이 없어도
환한 웃음으로 그대를 맞으리

천 년이 지나도
“궁전의 영광” 뭄타즈 마할은
샤 자한의 가슴속에
영원히 불타오르리라!

- Opening poem

Mumtaz Mahal

On the ground
The most beautiful palace of love
The Taj Mahal
Breathtakingly harmonious
Dazzling like a jewel

Oh, queen!
In your beautiful heart
A clear voice and a full charm
Unadorned personality and the outstanding intelligence
One day I miss you very much

Along the Yamuna River
Taj Mahal from Agra Castle
To find you
She wants to be with you
I'll go out

As if to say sorrow
Lying on the Taj Mahal
Her eyes
Without saying anything
I will welcome you with her bright smile

Even after a thousand years
“The Glory of the Palace” Mumtaz Mahal
In Shah Jahan’s heart
It will burn forever!

contents

제3부 알함브라의 추억

제4부 연인 자희태후

제5부 후지산

제6부 비엔티안

제7부 코타키나발루

제1부

백두산에 올라

아름다운 한반도의 산하 / 민족의 긍지
백두산!

백두산(白頭山) 천지(天池)

사방이 컴컴한 낮
매서운 추위와 바람이
휘몰아치더니
운해가 흩어지고
햇빛이 쏟아져 내리니
영롱한 물빛의 천지(天池)
보일 듯 말 듯…

천지의 물결이
신비의 색깔을 띠면서
무수히 바뀌어
남은 구름 바람에 흩어져
새로운 세계가 탄생하니
곧 한민족이니라

단군의 개국 신화가 깃든 곳
민족의 영원한 성산에
16폭 산수화가 병풍처럼
에워싸고
옥수경림(玉樹瓊林)이 있어
이곳이 신역(神域)이 아닌가!

백두대간을 따라
천상의 정원
백두산에
등정할 날을 기대해 본다.

Mount Baekdu, Heaven and Earth

A dark day all over the place
Bitter cold and wind
It swung
The sea of clouds is scattered
The sunlight pours down
The bright waters of heaven and earth
It seems like it can't be seen

The waves of heaven and earth
In the color of mystery
Changed countless times
The remaining clouds are scattered in the wind
A new world is born
Soon to be Korean

The place where the myth of Dangun's founding resides
To the eternal holy mountain of the nation
16 landscape paintings like a folding screen
Encircle
There is a clean tree forest
Isn't this the land of God!

Along mount range of Mt. Baekdu
Heavenly garden
On mount Baekdu
I look forward to the day when I can climb.

백두산에 올라

한민족의 얼이
스며있는 곳
백두산 여행의 출발점
연길시
60~70년대 한국을
다시 보는 듯…

옛 얘기를 들으며
덜커덩 끄릉끄릉
4시간의 버스 여정

울창한 숲
가도 가도 끝없는 밀림
대해수(大海樹)의 장관

1,200m 고지
버스 정류장에서
6인승 지프에 올라
10여 분 정상을
오르내릴 때
아찔한 순간의 연속

잔설이 성성한
고산지대 들꽃 군락을
쓰다듬거나
촬영도 할 수 없는 아쉬움

체감온도 영하 10도의
천문봉
혹한의 바람
톱니처럼 거친 봉우리

모였다가 흩어지는
구름 사이로
내리쬐는 햇살

천지의 짙푸른 수면에
기암이 어리어
그림 같은 풍경

천지가 나타나는구나

아름다운 한반도의 산하
민족의 긍지
백두산!

Climb Mt. Baekdu

The spirit of the Korean people
Where it seeps
The starting point of the trip to Mt. Baekdu
Yeongil city
Korea in the 60's and 70's
It's like seeing you again.

Listening to old story
A rattle of noise
4 hour bus journey

Dense forest
The endless jungle
A grand sight of the Great Sea

1,200m high
At the bus stop
Get on the 6 seater Jeep
10 minutes to the top
when it goes up and down
A series of dizzying moments

Snowy
A cluster of wild flowers in the alpine region
Stroking or
Too bad I can't even take a picture

The sensible temperature is minus 10 degrees
Cheonmunbong
Cold wind
Jagged peaks like a saw tooth

Gathering and scattering
Between clouds
Sun shining down

In the deep blue waters of heaven and earth
The strange rocks appear
A picturesque landscape

You see the heavens and earth

The beautiful Korean peninsula
National pride
Mt. Baekdu!

장백폭포

한 번 마시고 싶고
두 번 손을 넣어 만지고 싶고
세 번 발을 담가 보고 싶기도 한
천지의 맑고 푸른 물

백두산 정기를 받아
푸른 초원과 신비한 조화를 이루며
계곡으로 흐르다가

폭포의 꽃
장백 폭포에서
한 줄기 햇살에 비쳐
뜨는 무지개
여인의 속내를 보여 주는 듯
물보라를 흩날리네!

산기슭에서 솟구쳐 나오는 물
압록강과 두만강을 이루고
송화강으로 흘러드니
민족의 얼이 스며있네!

저 만주 대륙에
심양이 있고
연변이 있고
간도가 있지 아니한가!

고구려의 기상
한민족이여!

Jangbaek Falls

I want to drink once
I want to put my hand twice and touch it
I even wanted to dip my feet three times
Heaven and earth clear blue water

Receive the Mt. Baekdu spirit
In a mysterious harmony with the green meadows
Flowing into the valley

Waterfall flower
At Jangbaek waterfall
Reflected in a single ray of sunlight
Floating rainbow
It's like showing a woman's heart
I'm scattering sprays!

Water gushing from the foot of the mountain
It forms the Amnok River and the Tuman River
It flows into the Songhua River
The spirit of the nation is permeated!

On that continent of Manchuria
There is Shemyang
There is Yunbeoun
Isn’t There a Gando!

The conceit of Koguryeo
Korean people!

갠지스강 블루스

제2부

갠지스강 블루스

우리는 울지 않는다 / 슬퍼하지도 않는다
지금 여기는 / 우리의 고향이다.

죽녹원에서

바람이 불고
비가 내려
땅이 열린다

사각거리는 댓잎 소리와
때리는 빗방울 소리에
새로운 싹이 깨어나고
고동치는 생명력이
눈으로 틔어 솟아오른다

선비의 고결함이 서려 앉은
죽녹원에
혼을 묻으면

댓잎마다 젖어 드는 투명한 햇살이
돌아드는 바람에
죽림욕
죽로차
죽 향기

아, 마음에 휘어 감기는
생명력의 무한한 희열이
오솔길의 군상(群像) 위에
다가와 안기네!

At Juknokwon

Wind is blowing
It's raining
The ground is open

The sound of rustling leaves
To the sound of raindrops hitting
New sprouts are waking up
Pulsating vitality
It rises with my eyes

A scholar's nobility
In juknokwon
Bury your soul

The transparent sunlight soaking in every bamboo leaf
In the wind
Bamboo forest bath
Jukro Tea
Smell of porridge.

Oh, it's winding in my heart
The infinite bliss of vitality
On the group of statues on the path
Come and hug me!

갠지스강 블루스

이른 새벽 갠지스강
스산한 새벽 공기를 가르며
북적대는 바라나시 거리를 누빈다

미로 같은 골목길엔
개와 소, 사람 섞여 잠자고
큰 길가에는 거지들 좌우로 앉아
벌써 근무를 하고 있네

혼탁한 강물이 몸에 튈까 봐
간신히 배를 타고
예쁜 종이 꽃불을 물에 띄우며
잠시 주변을 살펴본다

시바 신을 숭배하는
최대의 성지 갠지스강
성스러운 강물에 목욕하고 빨래하고
이를 닦고 마시기도 한다

강변의 거지들
“사진 찍지 마세요.”
화장터 가까이서 ‘사진 촬영 금지’

그러나
우리는 울지 않는다
슬퍼하지도 않는다
지금 여기는
우리의 고향이다.

Ganges River Blues

Early dawn Ganges River
Parting through the hazy morning air
It is wandering the bustling streets of Varanasi

In a maze-like alleyway
Dogs, cows and people sleep together
Beggars sit left and right on the main road
I am already working

I'm afraid the turbid river water will splash on my body
Barely on the boat
Floating pretty paper flowers in the water
Take a look around

Worshiping the god of Shiva
Ganjis River, the most sacred place
Bathe and wash in the holy river
Brush your teeth and drink

Beggars by the river
“Don’t take pictures.”
‘No photography allowed’ near the crematorium

But
We don’t cry
I am not sad
Now, this is
It’s our hometown.

히든 밸리

누군가 말했던가

가고 싶은 곳

히든 밸리는
숨겨진 계곡이라고

스페인의 귀족들이
외국의 수상들이
스쳐 간 자연 휴양지

깨끗하고 맑은 공기
울창한 열대식물
천연 수영장과 폭포
달빛 찬란한 코코넛 숲속
밀림 속의 오솔길

아, 내가
태고로 잠시 돌아간 듯.

Hidden Valley

Did someone say

Where you want to go

Hidden Valley is
A hidden valley

Spain's nobles
Foreign awards
Skipped natural retreat

Clean and fresh air
Lush tropical plants
Natural pool and waterfall
In the moonlight shining coconut forest
Path in the jungle

Oh, I feel
It's like going back to ancient times for a while

산티아고 요새

이른 아침
일곱 빛깔을 가진 섬나라에
동녘 하늘의 여명이

자유를 갈망하는 자들의
멀고도 험한 여정

방황하고 헤매며
정처 없이 살아왔네

쓰러지고 넘어져도
독립을 위해

돌 성벽 쇠창살 아래
지하 감옥에서
괴로움도 주저함도 없이

희미한 어둠 속
작은 불빛을 목 말라 하며

파시그강 하구의
쓰레기처럼

물고기 떼의 호위 속에
바다로 떠내려가는 나의 심정
너는 알리라.

Fort Santiago

Early morning
To an island country with seven colored
The dawn of the eastern sky

Of those who long for freedom
A long and arduous journey

Wandering and wandering
She's been living aimlessly

Even if she falls and falls
For independence

Under the iron bars of the stone wall
In the dungeon
Without pain or hesitation

In the dim darkness
Thirsty for the little light

At the mouth of the Pasig River
Like trash

In the escort of a shoal of fish
My heart is drifting to the sea
You will know.

피나투보 화산

지난 세기말(末)

엄청난 진통 끝에
코발트 빛 하늘을 잉태한
맑은 칼데라호의 자태를
탄생시키고

이어 낳은
천상의 노천 온천

엄동설한을 피해 남하한
한국인을 위한 열대 지방 온천욕

뜨끈뜨끈한 유황 온천수에
몸을 담그고

아이 시원해
으이 시원해!

기기묘묘한 단층
자라다 만 나무들을 감상하며

어, 여기가
외계 횡성은 아닌가!

Pinatubo Volcano

End of last century

After great pain
Conceived of a cobalt light sky
Clear Caldera Lake
To give birth

Born
Heavenly open-air hot spring

Go south to escape the severe winter snow
Tropical hot springs for Koreans

In hot sulfuric spring water
Soaking up

Ah, cool
Oh, cool!

Bizarre faults
Admiring the growing trees

Uh, here
Isn't it an extraterrestrial Hoengseong?

발리 아궁산

발리는 인도네시아
17,509개의 섬 중 하나로
제주도의 2,7배
주민은 300여만 명으로
3,142m의 아궁산을
신성한 산으로 추앙한다

1963년 봄에 대분화로
큰 피해를 무릅쓰고
히말리아 산맥을
'신들의 정원'
아궁산은
'천국으로 가는 문'이라 하고

집 지을 때
대문을 아궁산 쪽으로
잠잘 때도
머리를 아궁산으로 향한다

멀리서도
낮게 보이는 아궁산은
우리에게 친근감을 주며
일출로도 유명한 신(神)의 산.

Bali Mount Agung

Bali Indonesia
As one of 17,509 islands
2,7 times that of Jeju Island
With over 3 million inhabitants
Mount Agung at 3142m
Revered as a sacred mountain

A major eruption in the spring of 1963
Despite great damage
Himalia Mountains
'Garden of the Gods'
Mount Agung
It's called "the door to heaven."

When building a house
Gate towards Mt. Agung
Even when sleeping
Head to Mount Agung

Even from afar
Mount Agung seen from below
Give us friendliness
The mountain of the gods is also famous for sunrise.

발리 봉선화

코코넛 넓은 잎사귀로
받침이나 그릇을 만들고
밤부 나뭇가지로
고정하여

봉선화로 장식하고
케이크, 떡, 과일 조각으로
짜낭을 만들어
제사장에 공급한다

제물로 쓰이는 봉선화
벼농사 짓듯
집집이 대량 생산하여
전날 저녁, 새벽에
시장에 공급한다

향을 피워
신들에게 행복을 구원하고
손톱에 물들여
향수를 느끼게 하네!

Bali Balsam

With coconut broad leaves
Make a pedestal or bowl
With chestnut twigs
By fixing

Decorate with balsam
Cake, rice cake and fruit slices
Make a napkin
Supply to the priest

Balsam used as a sacrifice
Like rice farming
House-to-house mass-produced
The night before, at dawn
Supply to the market

Burn incense
Save happiness to the gods
Dye your nails
It makes me feel nostalgic!

울루와트 비치

원시 암벽이 절벽을 이루고
인공 계단을 따라
오르고 내려가며 바라보는
짙푸른 바다

바위틈 사이로
자연이 만들어낸 공간으로
햇빛 쏟아져 들어오는 광경은
어디서도 보기 드물고

절벽 앞으로
끝없이 펼쳐진
에메랄드빛 바다는
자연이 빚어낸 천연 포토 존

바위로 연결된 틈 사이가
동굴처럼 생겨
거기에서 찍어내는
다양하고 멋진 인생 샷!

Uluwat Beach

The primitive rocks formations from cliffs
Along the artificial stairs
Looking up and down
Deep blue sea

Through the rocks
As a space created by nature
The sunlight pouring in
It's rare to see anywhere

Front of the cliff
Endlessly stretched out
The emerald sea
A natural photo zones created by nature

Between the cracks connected by rocks
Looks like a cave
Taken from there
Various and wonderful life shots!

갠지스강 블루스

제3부

알함브라의 추억

섬세한 손길 / 아라베스크 문양과
아라비아 서체 / 기하학적 무늬

에펠탑

에펠탑은
프랑스의 얼굴이며
문화의 상징이고
관광의 대명사이다

에펠탑은
방금 세수한
풋풋한 젊은이의 모습이며
손가락에 비취가락지를 낀
반려자이며
미래다

에펠탑은
파리의 조화로움을
대변이라도 하려는 듯
밤하늘을
청초하게 수놓는
별들과 함께
폭죽을 터트리며
모래알처럼 반짝이는
자동차 등불의 호위에

즐거움을 못 이긴 듯
밤마다
몸을 떨며
진저리친다.

The Eiffel Tower

The Eiffel Tower
The face of France
It's a symbol of culture
It is the epitome of tourism

The Eiffel Tower
Just washed
It's a young man with a good face
With a finger on the jade
A companion
Be the future

The Eiffel Tower
The harmony of Paris
As if it is trying to speak for
The night sky
Neatly embroidered
With the stars
In a firecracker
Glittering like a grain of sand

On the escort of a car lamp
As if it is not overjoyed
Every night
Trembling
The Eiffel Tower is fed up.

센강의 겨울

파리에는 센강이 흐르고
갖가지 모양의 다리 아래
유람선이 드문드문

세찬 바람
내리는 겨울비에
이따금 관광객들
옷깃을 여미며 서성거리네!

주변 주차장 많이 비어 있고
가까운 공원에서 바라다볼
전시공간 넓지 않네!

폭이 좁은 긴 강에는
긴 세월의 역사가 스며있고
찌푸린 날씨에도
마로니에 잎 흩날리는
강변 양안 둑 위에
산책객들 끊이지 않고
시상을 가다듬네!

찬란한 문화의 오아시스
센강에는
오늘도
강물처럼
세월이 흐르며
우리의 사랑도 흐른다.

Winter of the Seine River

The Seine River flows through Paris
Under the bridge of various shapes
Cruise ships are rare

A strong wind
In the winter rain
Occasionally tourists
I'm hanging around with my collar closed!

There's a lot of empty parking around here
Look at the nearest park
It's not a lot of exhibition space!

The long river with a narrow width
The history of the long years permeates
In spite of the frowning weather
The maronier leaves are scattered
On the bank of both banks of the river
The walkers are constantly
Remind the thought of poetry

An oasis of brilliant culture
In the Seine River
Today
Like a river
As the years pass
Our love flows.

개선문

3초 걸려 그윽한 눈빛으로
바라다본 개선문
인식하는 데는 잠깐이었네!

30초 걸려 꺼낸 카메라
파리의 얼굴, 개선문을
촬영하는 데는 잠깐이었네!

30분 걸려 도착한 개선문
엘리베이터를 타고
고문서 박물관까지
올라가는 데는 잠깐이었네!

30일 걸려 그리고 쓴
개선문의 그림과 글
보고 읽는 데는 잠깐이었네!

30년 걸려 건축한 개선문
나폴레옹의 장례행렬이
지나가는 데는 잠깐이었네!

Triumphal Arch

It took three seconds, with a deep look.
Triumphal Arch seen
It took a while to recognize!

Camera taken out after 30 seconds
The face of Paris, Triumphal Arch
It's been a while since we filmed!

Triumphal Arch arrived in 30 minutes
Take the elevator
To the Ancient Document Museum
It took a moment to get up!

It took 30 days and I wrote
The Paintings and Writings of the Triumphal Arch
It's a moment to watch and read!

The Triumphal Arch took 30 years to build
Napoleon's funeral procession
It was a moment since i passed by!

몽마르트르 언덕

전철역에서 나와
몽마르트르 언덕으로
정신없이
헐레벌떡 올라가니
좌우로 상가가 즐비하고
콘크리트 계단을 지나
저 위에 보이는
하얀 성당

여기가
어렸을 때부터
동경해 오던
그 몽마르트르 언덕인가!

거리 예술의 중심지이며
파리에서 가장 높은 언덕에서
시내를 내려다보며
시공(時空)을 넘어
자세히 보니

빅토르 위고가 글을 쓰고
고흐와 고갱과 피카소를 닮은
무명 화가들
화판에 초상화를 그리네!

몽마르트르 언덕 계단에 앉은 사람들
여기저기 서성거리는 보헤미안들을
다정하게 바라보네!

Montmartre Hill

Get out of the train station
To the Montmartre hills
Insidiously
I'm going up in a hurry
There are shops on the left and right
Through the concrete stairs
Look up there
White cathedral

Here
Ever since I was little
I've been longing for
That Montmartre Hill!

The center of street art
On the highest hill in Paris
Overlooking the city
Beyond time and space
I can see closely

Victor Hugo wrote
Like Van Gogh and Gauguin and Picasso
Unknown artists
You paint a portrait on the painting!

People sitting on the steps of Montmartre Hill
Bohemians wandering around
I look at you kindly!

아멜리아의 페냐성

파란 물감이 떨어질 듯
눈이 부시도록 드리워진 푸른 하늘 아래
우뚝 솟은 "영광의 에덴동산"
페냐성

신트라가 바라다보이는
매혹적인 마법의 성 테라스에
대서양의 해조음 가득 담고

로까 곶에서 불어오는 바람
파두의 즐거운 곡조를 싣고
왕궁의 무도장을 맴도네!

아름다운 숲속
동화 속 그림 같은 곳에
마지막 왕비 아멜리아가 남긴
화려함의 극치

기름진 음식과 호사스러운 복장
수많은 촛불을 밝힌
샹들리에 불빛 아래에서
귀족들과 춤을 출 때

한 노파는
바닷가 백사장에 앉아
돌아올 수 없는 어부 남편을 기다리며
슬픈 파두의 가락을 읊조렸으리라.

Amelia's Pena Castle

Blue paint seem to be falling
Under the dazzling blue sky
The towering "Garden of Eden of Glory"
Pena Castle

Overlooking Sintra
On the enchanting and magical castle terrace
Filled with the sounds of the Atlantic Ocean

Wind from Cape Roca
Carrying the pleasant tunes of Fado
Revolving around the ballroom of the royal palace!

Beautiful forest
In a place like a fairy tale
The last queen Amelia left behind
The extremes of glamour

Greasy food and luxurious attire
A large candlelight
Under the chandelier lights
When dancing with the nobles

An old woman
Sitting on the white sand beach
Waiting for a fisherman husband who can't return
She must have recite the melody of her sad fado.

알함브라의 추억

파란 하늘에 흰 구름
상쾌한 산속 공기를 머금고

그라나다 고원에 세워진
그윽하고 아름다운 옛 성
알함브라 궁전

흥망성쇠의 역사를
품 안에 간직한 채
온화함을 지니고
구릉 위에
태양처럼 빛나고 있구나

섬세한 손길
아라베스크 문양과
아라비아 서체
기하학적 무늬
색채의 황홀함은
이곳이 천상의 세계인가?

어디선가
“알함브라 궁전의 추억”이
들려오는 듯하다.

Memories of the Alhambra

White clouds in the blue sky
Breathe in the fresh mountain air

Built on the Granada Plateau
Quiet and beautiful old castle
Alhambra Palace

A history of rise and fall
Keeping it in my arms
With gentleness
On the hill
You are shining like the sun

Delicate touch
Arabesque pattern and
Arabic typeface
Geometric pattern
The ecstasy of color
Is this a heavenly world?

Somewhere
“Memories of Alhambra Palace”
It seems to be heard.

파블로 피카소

세기의 심장을 꿰뚫은
천재이자 미치광이인
금세기 최고의 예술가

미(美)는 인간의 철학이요
과학이며 문화임을 보여준
예언가

허물없는 솔직성과
모방할 수 없는 괴짜 기질이
매력의 근간을 이룬
선각자

작가와 여성에 대한
강렬한 우정과
뜨겁고 격정적인 사랑은
세기의 사랑을 만들고

보이지 않는 세계를
생각하며
생명력을 추구하여
만든 작품은
가장 미술가적인
세기의 예술가를 낳았네!

Pablo Picasso

Penetrating the heart of the century
Genius and madman
Best artist of this century

Beauty is a human philosophy
Science and culture
Prophet

Uncompromising honesty and
An inimitable geek
The basis of attraction
Planet

About writers and woman
Intense friendship
Hot and passionate love
Make the love of the century

The invisible world
Thinking
In pursuit of vitality
Her work is
Most artistic
The artist of the century was born!

톨레도

차창 밖으로 펼쳐지는 지평선
마을 중앙에 언덕이 있고
종탑이 있는 교회가
그림처럼 펼쳐진다

영화 '누구를 위하여 종을 울리나?'의
배경이 된 도시
천년의 역사가 그 자리에 머문
톨레도

좁고 미로 같은 골목
막히는가 하면
새로운 골목이 고개를 내밀고
넓어지는가 하면 좁아지는
울퉁불퉁 돌길은
중세도시에 들어선 기분

돈키호테와 엘 그레코
멋진 도자기와 금은 세공품이
즐비한 시가지

세계문화유산으로 지정된
톨레도는
오늘날에도
종교의 중심지로서
찬란히 빛나네!

Toledo

The horizon outside the car window
There's a hill in the center of town
The church with bell tower
Spread like a picture

From the movie "For Whom do you ring the Bell?"
City in the background
Thousands of years of history has stayed there
Toledo

Narrow, maze-like alley
If it gets blocked
A new alley sticks out its head
Widening and narrowing
The bumpy stone road
Feels like you are in a medieval city

Don Quixote and El Greco
Nice ceramics and gold and silver crafts
Lined streets

Designated as a world cultural heritage
Toledo is
Even today
As a center of religion
It shines brilliantly!

까보다로까

대륙의 영토가
대서양의 푸른 바다를 향해
이베리아반도를 통하여
힘차게 달리다가

유럽대륙의 최서남단
땅끝마을
로까 곶
해안 절벽 위에서
갑자기 용솟음치며 멎는다

계속 달리고 싶은 욕망은
많은 탐험가를 탄생 시켜
콜럼버스를 낳고
신대륙을 발견했으리라

평범해 보이는
바닷가 언덕에서
대서양의 끝없는 푸름을
한없이 바라보려니
미지의 세계로
항해하고 싶은 충동
억제하기 어려워라.

Cabo da Roca

The continental territory
Towards the blue ocean of the Atlantic Ocean
Through the Iberian Peninsula
Running vigorously

The southernmost tip of the European continent
Land end village
Cape Roca
On the coastal cliff
It suddenly springs up and stops

The desire to keep running
Birth of many explorers
Give birth to Columbus
It must have discovered a New continent

Ordinary looking
On the beach hill
The endless blue of the Atlantic Ocean
I want to look endlessly
Into an unknown world
The urge to sail
Hard to restrain.

갠지스강 블루스

제4부

연인 자희태후

책을 사랑하고 / 자연에 대한 섬세한 애착
예술에 대한 재주와 열정은 / 48년 권력자
서태후를 지켜 주었네!

만리장성에 서서

만리장성(萬里長城)에 오르다가
난간에 기대어
굽이굽이 펼쳐진 산등성이를
무심코 바라보다가
흠칫 놀랐다

누군가 닫힌 가슴
쉼 없이 열어젖히던
시절이 있었음에
그 누가 말하기를
"장성에 오르지 못하면, 호걸이 아니다"

"세계에서 가장 긴 무덤"
흔히 "하룻밤을 자도
만리장성을 쌓는다."
"사람이 장성보다 낫다."
라는 말이 끝없이 전개되나

세계 7대 불가사의라는
한마디가
장성을 더욱 돋보이게 하네!

Standing on the Great Wall of China

On the Great Wall
Lean against the railing
The ridge in which heel spreads
Look at it casually
I was surprised

Someone closed chest
I opened it without rest
There was a time
Who said
“If you don’t get to the Great Wall, you’re not a hero.

“The longest tomb in the world.”
“Even after a night’s sleep,
Build the Great Wall of China”
“People are better than the Wall”
There’s no end to this saying

The 7th Wonders of the World
This word is
Makes the Great Wall stand out even more!

이화원

곤명호를 관망하며
산수풍경을 보고 산책을 즐길 수 있는 장랑
넓은 호수에 두둥실 떠다니는 용선
호수 위에 비친 둘도 없는 절경
만수산 비탈의 불향각

연꽃과 버드나무가 어우러져
출렁이는 푸른 호수에
그 아름다움이 내려앉고
이름 모를 돌조각들은
여기저기에서
고무적인 산책길을 안내하네!

전각, 누각, 정자에서
꽃잎 차를 마시며
바라보는 4대 정원의 하나인

이화원은 하나의 시이고
수필이고
아름다운 소설이다

중국 천하에
사랑스러운 꽃과 나무 그리고 나비와 새
희귀하고 진귀한 보물
많은 궁인

아, 옛날은 가고
수양버들만 하늘하늘.

Summer Palace in Beijing

Watching lake Gonmyeong
Jangrang where you can enjoy a walk while looking at the landscape
A floating chartering in a wide lake
A spectacular view of the lake
The Bulhyang pavilion of the Slope of Mansu Mountain

Lotus and willows are combined
In a sloppy blue lake
With its beauty falling
The stones that don't know their names
All over the place
It's an encouraging walk

In the pavilions
Drinking petal tea
One of the four gardens

Summer Palace is a poem
An essay
It is a beautiful novel

Under China
Lovely flowers and trees and butterflies and birds
A rare and rare treasure
A lot of courtiers

Ah, the old days are gone
Only drooping willows are swing.

연인 자희태후

가난한 농부의 딸
예허나라 옥란은
산서성 낭낭원에서
유년 시절을 보내고
네 살 때 장치현에
양녀로 팔려 가
송영아란 이름을 얻는다

16세 때 예씨 성(姓) 중에서
궁녀로 선발되어 17세에 입궁
원명원의 초라한 하급 궁녀 방에서
출중한 미모와 재능, 예술적 감각으로
함풍제의 마음을 사로잡아
귀인에 책봉된다

20세에 의빈으로 승격하고
21세에 황태자를 출산하고
22세에 귀빈에 책봉
26세에 대청의 실질적 통치자가 되니
아마 그녀는 어떤 역경에도
굴하지 않는 의지의 소유자이리라

책을 사랑하고
자연에 대한 섬세한 애착
예술에 대한 재주와 열정은
48년 권력자
서태후를 지켜 주었네!

끊임없이 탐구하고
노력하는 습관
굳건한 의지력
과단성과 기민함으로
유서 깊고 광활한 대국
중화사상을 더욱 공고히 하고
이화원을 손수 설계하여
동지나 백성에게 사랑을 받았다

반세기 동안 권력을 휘두른
야망을 불태우며 불꽃처럼 살다간
여제 서태후(女帝西太后)는
국민을 진심으로 사랑했고
훌륭한 통치를 위해
부단히 노력한 인물이다

선한 의지와 순수한 동기에서
나온 사치와 오랜 철권독재는
격동기의 거대한 나라를 짊어진
어쩔 수 없는 결점으로 이해되리라

잔혹한 권력 세계에서
청조를 지켜 내야 한다는
책임감과 소명 의식이
그녀를 늘 고독하게 했으리라.

Lover, Empress Ja-hee

Daughter of a poor farmer
Yeheanara Okran
In Nangnang Garden, Shanxi Province
Spending her childhood
To Chang Chi-hyeon when I was four years old,
It's sold as a foster child
Get the name Song Yeong-a

Of Ye's surname at the age of 16
She was selected as a court lady and entered the palace at the age of 17
In Won Myeong-won's humble lower court room
With a good beauty, talent, and artistic sense
Captivate the heart of Hampungje
To become a noble woman

He was promoted to Euibin at the age of 20
She gave birth to a crown prince at the age of 21
An honored guest at the age of 22
At the age of 26, the real ruler of the Great Qing Dynasty
Maybe she's got no problem with any difficulty
She will be the owner of undaunted will

I love books
A delicate attachment to nature
The knack and passion for art
48 Years of Power
You protected Cixi!

Constantly exploring
A habit of effort
A firm willpower
With exaggeration and agility
A historic and vast nation
To further consolidate the idea of neutralization
By hand designing the Summer Palace in Beijing
She was loved by her comrades and people

A half century of power wielding
You know, if you burn your ambitions and live like a flame
Seo Tae-hoo is a Woman Empress
She loved the people with all her heart
For good rule
She's a woman of constant effort

In good will and pure motive
The luxury and the long ironclad dictatorship
A turbulent country
We will understand it as an inevitable fault

In a world of brutal power
To protect the Qing Dynasty
Sense of responsibility and vocation
She must have made her always lonely.

자금성

중국의 상징이요
고동치는
천안문광장의 위용
대륙의 위대한 지도자 모택동 영정

거대한 북경의 고궁
천자가 군림했던 곳
명·청 시대의 조화(造花)
주황색 기와지붕
크고 붉은 둥근 기둥
어도를 밟아 신무문까지
찬란한 황금색 구중궁궐

태화전 어전에서
오체투지(五體投地)의 만조백관
역사 속으로 묻히고

세계 제일의 궁전에서
세계 제일의 대국을 이룩하려는
중국인의 의지가 엿보이네!

황제도 백성으로 돌아가고
열린 오문을 통하여
누구라도 어도를 걷고 있는
중화인민들
지금 세계를 향해
무소불위의 기업 권력을 휘두르네!

Forbidden City

A symbol of China
Throbbing
The prestige of Tiananmen Square
The great leader of the continent, Mao Tse-tung

A huge Beijing palace
The place where the Emperor reigned
The harmony of the Ming and Qing era
Orange tile roof
A large red column
Take the path of the king
A glorious golden palace

At a Royal council in the Taehwajeon
A high tide white crown consisting of Five Body Tuji
Buried in history

In the world's greatest palace
To make the world's greatest nation
You can see the will of the Chinese!

The emperor returns to his people
Through an open Meridian Gate
Anyone walking on the path of the king
Chinese people
Towards the world now
We wield the power of an unparalleled corporation!

상하이 서커스

인간의 능력을 최대한으로 끌어내어
올림픽을 축소한 듯한
우아한 여러 종목의 시(詩)
어릿광대를 통해

배경 음악
곤봉 체조
접시 돌리기
세 사람의 아크로바트 파워
균형 잡기 묘기
훌라후프 돌리기
날라서 원 통과하기
자전거 타기 묘기
손에 땀을 쥐게 하는
아슬아슬한 오토바이 쇼

"와, 세상에"

관중의 시선을 꼼짝 못 하게 붙잡는
이 다양한 곡예가
기쁨과 슬픔이 놀라움과 긴장으로 바뀌어
상하이를 세계 중심의 도시로
나아가
중국 경제를 이끌어 가네!

Shanghai Circus

Unleash the full potential of human beings
Looks like the Olympics have been reduced
Poetry of various elegant events
Through the clown

Background music
Club gymnastics
Turn the plate
Three acrobat powers
Balancing stunts
Hula hoop spinning
Flying through the circle
Bicycle riding stunts
Sweaty hand
A breathtaking motorcycle show

"Wow, my God"

Capturing the audience's gaze
These various acrobats
Joy and sadness turn into surprise and tension
Shanghai as a center of the world
Furthermore
Leading the Chinese economy!

항주 서호(西湖)

물안개 자욱한 서호의 겨울
을씨년스럽고
온종일 이슬비 내리니
서운함과 아쉬움이
머릿속을 스친다

바다 같은 호수에서
항주 미인 서시를 그리고
이태백의 시를 낭송하며
주변 나라들의 흥망성쇠에
유람선이 역사 속으로 흐르는 듯

늘 산책하고 싶은 호숫가
통기타를 메고
하늘거리는 수양버들
호수에 비친 석등의 불빛
물 위에 어리는
달 밝은 밤을 노래한다

아침이든
저녁이든
눈 오는 날이든
호수 주변을 다니며
가끔 유람선도 타고
카메라로 사진도 촬영해보면
그 옛날 선현들이 즐겼을
서호의 4계절 풍광이
'찰랑찰랑' 물결 소리와 함께
가슴을 스쳐 지나가네!

Hangzhou West Lake

The misty winter of west Lake
Gloomy weather
It's been drizzling all day long
The sadness and the regret
It goes through my mind

In a lake like the sea
Missing Hangzhou beauty, Searcy
In reciting Lee Tae-Baek's Poetry
In the rise and fall of the surrounding countries
As if a cruise ship were flowing into history

The lakeside I'd always like to take a walk
With an acoustic guitar
A fluttering willow
The light of the stone lamps in the lake
Swirling on the water
Sing the moonlight night

Morning or not
In the evening
On a snowy day
Around the lake
Sometimes we'll take a cruise ship
I'll take a picture with the camera
The ancient sages would have enjoyed
The four Seasons of the West Lake
With the sound of the wave
Passing through your chest!

동방명주탑

광활한 대지
넘치는 인구
중화 경제의 상징
아시아 최고의 관제탑
푸둥의 동팡밍주

순수 자국 자본으로 만들어진 송신탑
세계에서 가장 빠른 속도로 운행되며
기네스북에 등재된 엘리베이터

전망대에서 내려다본 경제 수도
상하이의 찬란한 건축문화에 압도된 사람들
신음에 가까운 탄성
황푸강 주변으로
천지가 개벽할 마천루의 위용

와이탄을 바라보니
야간에는 유람선이
고속도로를 달리는 자동차처럼
황홀하게 줄을 이어
시각적 쾌락의 극치를 이룬다

정상으로 발돋움하려는
중국 경제가
영화처럼 펼쳐지는 듯

차이나 시대가 오고 있는가!

Oriental Pearl Tower

A vast earth
A full population
Symbol of the Chinese economy
The best control tower in Asia
Oriental Pearl of pudong

A transmission tower made of pure domestic capital
It runs at the fastest speed in the world
Elevator listed in Guinness Book

Economic Capital looking down from the observatory
People overwhelmed by Shanghai's brilliant architectural culture
A groaning elasticity
Around the Huangpu River
The majesty of a skyscraper that will open the heavens and the earth

Looking at Waitan
At night, a cruise ship
Like a car on a highway
Line up in ecstasy
The extreme of visual pleasure is accomplished

A normal step
Chinese economy
Like it's a movie.

The China Age is coming!

매헌누각(梅軒樓閣)

이 아담한 한옥이
어디에 있는지
우리는 압니다

보이지 않는 곳에
여기저기
빛나는 애국정신이 있음을
우리는 압니다

당신을 만들고
당신을 빛내 준
당시의 민족의 아픔을
우리는 압니다

당신이 구국의 이상을 찾으러
어둠을 헤치고
압록강을 건너는 긴 여정이
민족의 횃불이 된다는 것을
우리는 압니다

당신은 보이는 모습이
전부가 아님을
우리는 압니다

당신의 감춰진 모습도
아름답다는 것을
우리는 압니다.

Maeheon Pavilion

This little Korean traditional house
Where is it?
We know

In an Invisible place
Here and there
That there is a shining patriotism
We know

Make you
Made you shine
The suffering of the nation at that time
We know

You're looking for the ideal of national salvation
Through the darkness
The long journey across the Yalu River
That it will be a national torch
We know

What you look like
Not everything
We know

Your hidden image
That it's beautiful
We know.

화청지

서안 리 산 아래
양질의 온천수가
샘솟는다는 화청지

철철 넘치는 온천수로
피부를 가꿔
세기의 사랑을 이끈
양귀비와 현종의 로맨스 무대

장한가 가무극의 야외무대
봄 여름 가을이 성수기인
초현대식 공연장

양귀비가 서시, 왕소군, 초선과 함께
중국의 4대 미인으로,
그녀의 유명한 석상으로
더욱더 유명해진 화청지(华清地).

Hwacheongji

Under Mount Rhee, Seoan
Good quality hot spring water
Hwacheongji that springs up

Filled hot spring water
Make your skin look after
Led the love of the century
Poppy and Hyunjong's Romance Stage

The outdoor stage of the Janghanga
Spring summer autumn is the peak season
Ultramodern performance hall

Poppy with Searcy, Wangsogoon, Choseon
The four most beautiful women in China,
As a famous statue of her
The more famous Hwacheongji!

갠지스강 블루스

제5부

후지산

굽이굽이 맑은 계곡 / 환상의 후지오호(富士五湖)
모두가 후지산을 우러르네.

후지산

후지산(富士山)
홀로 우뚝
구름 덮인 봉우리들
모양도 각각
오색 빛 흐른다

세속에 찌든 마음
이곳에서 모두 씻겨

천상의 사람
천하의 자연
세상 시끄러움 끊고
열도의 동쪽 불의 영봉(靈峰)
창공 위에 올라 있네

지날 때마다
솟는 해 바라보며
세상 사는 번뇌
느끼지 못하고
가만히 살펴보니
수많은 봉우리에 빼어난 사계(四季)

굽이굽이 맑은 계곡
환상의 후지오호(富士五湖)
모두가 후지산을 우러르네.

Mount Fuji

Mt. Fuji
Stand tall alone
Cloud-covered peaks
Shape each
Colorful light flows

A worldly mind
All washed up here

A heavenly man
The nature of the world
Cut off the noise In the world
A sacred mountain of the Eastern Fire of the Islands
It's on the blue sky

Every time it passes
Looking up at the rising sun
The world's troubles
Unfeelingly
I'm just looking at it
Four great seasons on numerous peaks

A clear bended valley
Fuji five lakes of fantasy
Everyone looks up to Mount Fuji.

벳푸 온천 지옥

온천 관광의 대명사 "벳푸 온천 지옥"을 순례해 보니,
'산은 후지산이요, 바다는 세토, 온천은 벳푸'라고 눈에 띄네.

첫 번째 관문, 도깨비 대머리 지옥에 들어서니,
에메랄드빛 물이 바다처럼 보이고 온천수로 만두도 찌네. 하지만, 회색의 진흙이 끓어올라 작은 구형을 만들어내는데
마치 삭발한 스님의 머리를 연상케 하고,
돌에서 연기가 모락모락 피어오르니 음습하여 진짜 지옥 같네.

두 번째 관문, 바다 지옥에 들어서니,
억새로 만든 지붕이 두메산골 오막살이 집들을 연상케 하고, 주변에는 뜨거운 온천수를 먹고 자란 나무가 사시사철 푸르러 이곳이 천국이지 어찌 지옥이란 말인가!

세 번째 관문, 산지옥에 들어서니, 지하에서 솟구친 진흙이 식으면서 산을 닮아 사방에서 하얀 수증기가 푹푹 솟아오르니 영락없는 지옥이라.

네 번째 관문, 솥 지옥에 들어서니,
수증기로 밥을 지어 신에게 바쳤다는데,
'솥 지옥에서 온천수를 마시면 10년 젊어진다' 하여 두 잔을 마셨네.

다섯 번째 관문, 도깨비산 지옥에 들어서니,
보르네오섬의 가옥을 옮겨 와 온천 열을 이용해 악어를 사육하여 지옥을 만들었다.
우글거리는 악어들의 사투를 보니 지옥이 따로 없네.

여섯 번째 관문, 흰 연못 지옥에 들어서니,
무색투명한 온천수가 연못으로 흘러들면 청백색으로 변하여 신비감을 준다.
95도 온천수가 압력이 서서히 낮아지면 독특한 색이 나타나며,
이 온천 열을 이용해 열대어를 기르고 있다.
아마존 식인물고기 피라니아도 볼 수 있어 가장 조용하고 자연친화적인 온천이다.

일곱 번째 관문, 피 연못 지옥에 들어서니,
고온, 고압의 화학반응을 일으켜 온천물이 핏빛처럼 보인다고 해서 피 연못이다.
이 진흙이 피부미용에 좋아서 비누로 만들어 판매된다.
단풍이 좋은 산책로로 조성되어 데이트하기 그만이다. 피바다처럼 보이지만, 이 진흙 또한 일본에서도 알아준다고 한다.

여덟 번째 관문, 소용돌이 지옥에 들어서니,
피 연못 지옥 바로 옆에 있어 일명 회오리 지옥이라고도 한다.
30분 정도 지하에서 끓다가 갑자기 용천수가 탁 튀어나와 온천지역임을 실감 나게 해준다.

150도 열탕이 50m 솟는데, 데일까 봐 위쪽을 막아 놓았다.
간헐천의 진수를 느낀다.

규수 벳푸 지역의 온천은 원천 수와 용출량에 있어 일본 제일이자 현존하는 거의 모든 수질의 온천을 4천여 개나 보유하고 있어 온천 여행의 백미라 할 수 있다.
또한, 성분에 따라 다양한 색상의 뜨거운 온천과 증기가 분출되는 8개 코스에서 독특한 온천 경험을 할 수 있어, 관광은 물론 온천 열로 채소, 화초 등 농사도 지을 수 있다.

Beppu Onsen Hell

When I went on pilgrimage to "Beppu Onsen Hell", which is the synonymous with hot spring tourism, it stood out as "The mountain is Fuji Mountain, the sea is Seto, and hot spring is Beppu."

Entering the First Gateway, the Goblin Bald Hell,
Emerald water looks like the sea and the hot spring water steams the dumplings. However, the gray mud boils and forms small spheres
Reminds me of a monk with a shaved head,
The smoke is rising from the stone, and it's so wet and it's like hell.

Entering the Second Gateway, in the Sea Hell,
The roof made of a billion won reminds me of the houses of Dumesan Gol, and the trees that grew up eating hot spring water around are green, so this is heaven.

As you enter the Third Gateway, in the Mountain Hell, the mud that rose from the ground cooled and resembled the mountain white steam rises up, and it is hell without a heart.

When I entered the Fourth Gate, the pot, in hell, he made rice with steam and gave it to God,
I drank two glasses, "I drink hot spring water from the pot hell and I will be 10 years younger."

Entering the Fifth Gate, the Goblin Mountain Hell,
They moved the house of Borneo Island and used the heat of the hot spring to raise crocodiles to make hell.The struggle of the crocodiles is a hell of a hell.

Entering the Sixth Gate, White Pond Hell,
When the colorless transparent hot spring water flows into the pond, it turns blue and white, giving a mystery.
When the pressure of 95 degrees hot spring water gradually decreases, a unique color appears,
The hot spring heat is used to raise tropical fish.
You can also see the Amazon cannibal pirania, the quietest, most nature-friendly spa.

Entering the Seventh Gate, the pool of blood hell,
It is a blood pond because it causes chemical reactions of high temperature and high pressure and the hot springs look like blood. This mud is good for skin beauty and is made into soap and sold. It is a walkway with good maple

leaves and it is enough to date. It looks like a bloodbath, but this mud is also known in Japan.

Entering the Eighth Gateway, Whirlpool Hell,
It is also called the whirlwind hell because it is right next to the blood pond hell.
It boils underground for about 30 minutes, and suddenly the water of the spring pops out and makes you realize that it is a hot spring area.
The 150-degree heat is 50 meters high, and I blocked it up because I thought it was burnt.
I feel the essence of the geyser.

The hot springs in the Kyusu Beppu area are the first in Japan in terms of source number and elution volume.
We have about 4,000 hot springs of almost all water quality
It is the hlghlight of a hot spring trip.
In addition, in eight courses where hot springs and steam of various colors erupt according to the component
You can experience a unique hot spring experience, and you can build farming such as vegetables and flowers with hot spring heat as well as sightseeing.

갠지스강 블루스

제6부

비엔티안

순수로 물든 숲은 / 루앙프라방과 방비엥을
정겹고 포근하게 / 에워싸고

비엔티안

화려하지만 소박한
라오스의 얼굴 비엔티안은
달의 도시

순수로 물든 숲은
루앙프라방과 방비엥을
정겹고 포근하게
에워싸고

유럽과 아시아 문화가
잘 어우러져
평화로운 분위기가
관광객의 발길을 붙잡는 것을

땀 흘려가면서라도
그 뜨거운 만남을 위해
훌쩍 날아가리라
비엔티안으로.

Vientiane

A gorgeous but simple
Laos' face Vientiane
City of the moon

The forest dyed with pure water
Luang Prabang and Vangvieng
In a hearty and warm cozy
Encircling

European and Asian cultures
In good harmony
The peaceful atmosphere
Hold on to the tourist

In sweating
For that hot meeting
I'll fly away
To Vientiane.

블루라군

투명한 침묵이
몇 바퀴 허공을 맴돌 듯
잠시 주춤거리다가
한번 호흡을 가다듬으면
도도한 폭포수처럼 떨어져
보는 이의 마음을 사로잡는다

규모는 작아도
수심 5m의 열대 해(海)를
떠올리게 하는 독특한
에메랄드빛 물결

낭만적인 그네와 다이빙대는
인간문화의 뿌리를 찾아
마지막 원시인을 보는 듯

오늘도 이상향을 찾아
꿈꾸는
라오스 관광의 백미(白眉).

Blue Lagoon

A transparent silence
A few laps in the air
I hesitate for a moment
Once you've worked your breath
It falls like a waterfall
Capture the heart of the viewer

Even if it is small
The tropical sea of the depth of 5m
A unique reminder
Emerald wave

The romantic swing and the diving board
Find the roots of human culture
As if to see the last primitive

I'm looking for a vision today
Dreaming
The highlight of tourism in Laos.

팟투사이

팟투사이는
비엔티안의 얼굴이며
문화의 상징이고
수직 활주로의 대명사이다

팟투사이는
방금 세수를 한
순수한 젊은이의 모습이며
수려한 차림의 반려자이고
미래다

팟투사이는
일몰의 조화로움을
말하려는 듯
박하 향이 날 것 같은 푸른 물에
들뜬 마음을 사방으로 흩날리고

청초하게 수놓는
밤하늘의 별들과 함께
폭죽을 터트리며

메콩강에 비치는
자동차 등불에
기쁨을 못 이긴 듯
밤마다
승리의 춤을 춘다.

Patuxai

Patuxai is
Vientiane's face
It's a symbol of culture
It's a synonymous of a vertical runway

Patuxai is
Just washed your face
A pure youth
He's a handsome companion
Be the future

Patuxai
The harmony of sunset
As if to say
In the blue water in which the mint smells
I scatter my mind all over the place

Neatly embroidered
With the stars in the night sky
In a firecracker

Shining on the Mekong River
On a car lights
As if I had not overjoyed
Every night
Dance the victory.

방비엥 짚라인

끝없이 공간으로 이어지는
외줄 타기

온 힘을 쏟아
무한에 가까운 공간 속에
자신을 응집시키려
안간힘을 쓴다

줄 타고 날아가
대롱대롱
위태롭게
심장이 멈추겠네

모든 기억에서 떨어져
공간으로 날아간다

무한 속
무(無)로 이어지는 이 공간에서
갱년기의 호르몬 변화가
나를 일으켜 세우네.

Vangvieng Zipline

Endlessly leading to space
Single line riding

With all your strength
In the space nearing infinity
To cohere oneself
Struggle hard

Fly on a tightrope
Daelong daelong
Dangerously
My heart will stop!

Get away from all the memories
Fly into space

Infinite genus
In this space that leads to nothing
Hormonal changes in menopause
You're raising me up.

파잔 의식

하루 정도는 견딘다
나뭇등걸이 삐걱거리고
바닥이 솟구쳐 오르고
하늘이 맴을 돌지만
하루 일쯤으로 기억한다

창밖엔
불러도 대답 없는 그림자
상처받은 모성애
영혼 박탈

시간이 흐를수록
가물거리는 요람의 기억
하얗게 비워지는 자아

야성의 시간이 멈춘 후에도
오직 따그로는
세월과 함께 춤을 춘다.

Fazan Ritual

I endure for a day or so
The wooden rack is creaking
The floor is rising
The sky is hovering
I remember about a day

Out the window
A shadow without answer
Hurt motherhood
Soul deprivation

As time goes by
Memories of Cradle Blinking
A white emptied ego

Even after the wild time stopped
Only Tagro
Dancing with the years

호찌민 박물관

베트남 사람들은
국민적인 신(神)이라 해도 좋을 만큼
호찌민을 아끼고 사랑하며
추앙한다

빛을 가져오는 사람
호찌민은
승천할 때 유산이 없으며
전용 자동차도 손님을 위해
쓰이고
국민을 더 사랑하고자
평생 독신으로 살다 갔다

탁월한 정치 지도력을 통해
새로운 역사를 창조해낸
영원한 민족주의자

낫과 망치와 별을 바라보며
오토바이 군무가
경적을 울리며 달려가듯
국가가 발전하고 있다

어쩌면
거리가 멀고 열대지방인데도
습성과 풍습이 비슷하고
한국인과 많이 닮았다.

Ho Chi Minh Museum

Vietnamese people
It's like a national god
Cherishing and loving Ho Chi Minh
Be admired

The one who brings light
Ho Chi Minh
There is no legacy in ascending
Private cars for guests
Use
To love the people more
He has been single all his life

Through outstanding political leadership
A new history
An eternal nationalist

Looking at the sickle, the hammer, the stars
A motorcycle dancer
Like a horn running
The state is developing

Maybe
It's a long distance, it's tropical
We have similar habits and customs
They look a lot like Koreans.

일주사(一柱寺)

옛날 옛적에

베트남 리 왕조시대에
후사를 못 보던 왕이
보리수나무 밑에서
기도를 하던 중
길몽을 꾸었네!

그 보리수 앞에
연못을 조성하고
월남의 국화
연꽃을 형상화한
일주 탑을 지었네!

붉은 가사 어깨 걸친
관음보살
1,000일 기도 후
왕자를 얻었네!

연꽃 닮은 가람(伽藍)
비좁은 계단
마루 앞뜰
중생들로 틈이 없네!

One Column Temple

In the old days

During the Li dynasty of Vietnam
The king who never saw his heir
Under the bodhi tree
In prayer
You've got a lucky dream!

In front of the bodhi tree
To build a pond
Chrysanthemum in Vietnam
Lotus-shaped
You built one column tower!

Red surplice-shouldered
The Buddhist Goddess of Mercy
1,000 Days After Prayer
You got a prince!

A temple resembling lotus flowers
Cramped staircase
Floor front yard
There's no gap for the people!

깟바섬의 겨울

아열대 풍의 해수욕장이
3개나 이웃해 있는 곳

하롱베이 섬들의 왕
깟바섬의 겨울은
조용한 휴양지

최신형 새 호텔의 포근함
1박의 여유

롱차우 정상에서 보는
불그스레한 태양의 일출

아슬아슬한 깟꼬 해변 절벽 길 위로
한참 걸어가는 아찔함

야자수 그늘에서
작렬하는 7월의
바닷가를 그리며
맹그로브 숲 가의
가녀린 꽃들을 바라본다

저녁 식사 후
불꽃놀이에
내 마음 젊게
멀리 펼쳐 본다.

Winter on Cat Ba Island

Subtropical beaches
Three neighboring places

King of the Halong Bay islands
Winter on the island of Cat Ba
A quiet resort

The warmth of the newest hotel
A night's free

View from the top of Long Chow
The sunrise of the reddish sun

Over the narrow Katko beach cliff path
A long walk of dizziness

In the shadow of palm trees
A raging July
Missing the beach
Mangrove forest
Look at the delicate flowers

After dinner
In a fireworks display
Keep my heart young
I look it far away.

노트르담 대성당

그 옛날
프랑스 식민지 시대인
19세기 후반에 건설된
높이 40m의 종탑

마르세유 항구에서
직접 공수한
화려한 창문과 붉은색 벽돌

천년 역사의 호찌민을
동양의 파리로
거듭나게 한 대성당

주변 벽돌담에는
베트남의 역사를
말해주는
다양한 벽화가
지나가는 사람의
발걸음을 멈추게 한다.

Notre Dame Cathedral

The old days
French colonial period
Built in the late 19th century
A 40m high bell tower

At the port of Marseille
Airlifted directly
Colorful windows and red bricks

A Ho Chi Minh of millennium history
To the eastern paris
A cathedral born again

The surrounding brick walls
History of vietnam
Telling
Various mural paintings
A passing person
Make your stop walking.

호찌민 그리스도상

지붕이 빨갛게 보이는
호찌민 붕따우

바이두아 해변에서
올려다본
197m의 뇨산 위에
36m의 거대 예수상

누구나 쉽게
올라갈 수 있도록
10cm 높이의 811계단을
못 오를 리 없건만
이를 모르는 사람들
지레짐작
등정을 외면한다

예수를 만나고 내려온
70대의 여행객을 보고
부럽다고
대단하다고
축하 인사를 한다.

The Statue of Ho Chi Minh Christ

Red-looking roof
Ho Chi Minh Bung Tau

On the beach in Baidua
Look up
On 197m high the uric acid
A giant statue of Jesus at 36m

Anyone can easily
To go up
10cm high 811 steps
There's no way you can't climb it.
People who don't know this
Giraffe guessing
Avoid climbing

Came down from the meeting Jesus
Seeing travelers in their seventies
I envy you
It's great
Congratulations.

오토바이 군무

경제 도시 호찌민시
너무 많은 오토바이 떼에
묻혀
보이지 않는 택시

앞뒤 좌우로
붙어 달리는
오토바이 군무(群舞)에
집단이 움직이는 듯

신호등도 없이
무 사고율을
자랑하는 오토바이들

무질서 속에
질서가 존재하는
삶의 향수이자
오토바이 천국.

Motorcycle Group Dancing

Economic city of Ho Chi Minh
Too many motorcycles
Buried
Invisible taxi

From side to side
Running close
In the motorcycle group dancing
As if a group were moving

Without traffic lights
Accident-free rate
Bragging motorcycles

In disorder
Order-existing
The nostalgia of life
Motorcycles paradise.

무이네 사막

호찌민 근교
무이네 사막

사막의 오아시스처럼
작은 사막 언덕
깨끗한 모래 먼지로
그 외관을 뽐내고

한낮엔 이글거리는 햇볕
습기가 없고
바람이 불 땐
눈뜨기가 어려워
특수 안경을 쓰고
썰매도 타며

4륜 바이크로 힘차게
봉우리를 넘나들며
사막에서
여행의 열정을 불태운다.

Mui Ne Desert

Ho Chi Minh suburb
Mui Ne Desert

Like the oasis of the desert
A small desert hill
With clean sand dust
Showing off that look

A glowing sun in the middle of the day
Without moisture
When the wind blows
It's hard to open your eyes
Wearing special glasses
And we rode sleds

With a four-wheel bike
Across the peak
In the desert
Ignite the passion of travel.

요정의 샘물

붉은 모래로
흙탕물처럼 보이지만
흐르는 시냇물은 맑다

맨발로
부드러운 모래를 밟고
거슬러 올라가니
발을 마사지하는 듯

365일 물이 마르지 않아
붙여진
요정의 샘물

걸을 때
자박자박 물소리
양옆에 끝없이
붉게 보이는 모래 산

계속 걷다 보면
밀림을 지나
그랜드 캐니언에 온 듯.

Fairy's Spring

With red sand
It looks like muddy water
The flowing stream is clear

Barefoot
Step on the soft sand
Go back
Like a foot massage

365 days of water is not dry
Attached
Fairy spring water

When walking
The sound of beating water
On both sides of the road
A red-looking sand mountain

If you keep walking
Through the jungle
Like being in the Grand Canyon.

갠지스강 블루스

제7부

코타키나발루

멋진 해넘이와 / 파란 하늘//
주홍빛 노을이 아름다운 / 석양의 섬.

코타키나발루

인천공항에서
4시간쯤 지나
도착한
코타키나발루는
동남아의 파라다이스

한국의 자연환경과 비슷한
말레이시아
키나발루산 아래
사바주

멋진 해넘이와
파란 하늘

주홍빛 노을이 아름다운
석양의 섬.

Kotakinavalu

At Incheon Airport
About four hours later
Arrived
Kotakinabalu is
Paradise in Southeast Asia

Similar to the natural environment of Korea
Malaysia
Under Mt. Kinavalu
Sabah province

With a wonderful sunset
Blue sky

A beautiful scarlet sunset
The sunset Island.

천상의 계단

바다에서 육지로
육지에서
천상의 계단을 타고

구름 위로
하늘로 오르고 싶다

바다는 파랗다
하늘도 파랗다

그 푸른 세계가
넓고
신비스러워

몸은 여기에 살면서
마음은 미래의 세상에
온 듯하네!

Stairway to heaven

From the sea to the land
On land
Climb the stairway to heaven

Over the clouds
I want to rise to the sky

The sea is blue
The sky is blue too

The blue world
Wide
Mysterious

The body lives here
The mind is the world of the future
It seems to have come!

그물침대

먼 옛날
열대지방 원주민들이
사용한 해먹

강우량이 많고
습도가 높아

바닷가 기둥이나
나무 그늘 같은 곳에
끈을 매어놓고

누워서
휴식을 취할 수 있도록
만들어진 그물

세월이 흘러
배
피서지
달착륙선에서도
쓰이는 그물침대!

Net Bed

A long time ago
The natives of the tropics
Used hammock

Heavy rainfall
High humidity

A beach post
In a place like a shade of wood
Strap it up

Lying down
Rest is had
Made net

Year pass
Ship
Summer resort
On the lunar lander
Used hammock!

야자수 전망대

넓은 모래사장에서
해수욕을 즐기다가

원시림이 잘 조성된
바닷가

야자수로 지어진
2층 전망대에서

라야라야비치의 풍광을
한눈에 담는다

전망대에서 바라본
최고로 멋진 석양을 그리며

어디론가 가야지
가야지

가슴으로 끝없이
상상의 나래를 편다.

Palm Tree Observatory

On the wide sandy beach
Enjoing the sea bathing

Well-preserved forest
Seaside

Built of palm trees
On the second floor observatory

The view of Rayaraya Beach
Put at a glance

View from the observatory
Drawing the best sunset

Where are we going?
I have to go

Endlessly with chest
Have a vision of imagination.

이슬람 사원

멀리서도
웅장하게 보인다

원형의 본관
떠받치는 육중한 첨탑
부속 건물이
우아하고 장엄하다

넓은 공간의 내부에는
붉은색, 초록색의 양탄자가
깔려 있고

검소해 보이는 실내를
맨발로 다녀

엄숙하면서도
인간미가 넘친다.

A mosque

Even from a distance
Looks magnificent

Round main building
A heavy spire to support
The annexed building
Be elegant and majestic

Inside the wide space
Red, green carpets
Laid down

A frugal looking interior
Go barefoot

Solemnly
It is full of humanity.

열대 고양이의 오수

여기저기 돌아다니는
열대 고양이가

식탁 테이블 위에서
오수(午睡)에 빠져 있다

감히 밥상 위에서
사람처럼 잠을 자다니

지나가는 사람들의 헛기침 소리에
눈을 떴다가는 감고
얼굴을 돌리는 척 다시 잔다

열대 고양이는 동네 사람과 같이 있다
한 가족일까?

한참 만에 돌아와 보니
그때도 자고 있다.

A Tropical Cat Nap

All over the place
Tropical cats

On the table
Be taking a nap

Dare to sit on the table
Sleeping like a human being?

Hearing the noise of passing people
Opening your eyes, closed them You sleep again, pretending to turn your face

Tropical cat is with people in the neighborhood
A family?

They came back in a while
The cat is sleeping then.

나나문 반딧불이

어스름이 피어오르는
깜깜한
맹그로브 숲속에

작은 반딧불이가
수를 놓는다

반짝반짝
빛이 모여 추는 춤은
어느 불빛보다
내 마음을 흔들고

손전등 불빛 따라
점멸하는 불빛으로

뱃길을
안내하는 의로움!

Nanamoon Firefly

Dusk-blooming
Dark
In the mangrove forest

Little firefly
Embroider

Gleamingly
The dance of light
Than any light
Shaking my mind

By the flashlight
In flashing light

On the boat
The righteousness to guide!

수중 탐사

망망대해
갑판 위에서
어두컴컴한 바다
한가운데로 뛰어내린다

생명줄에 의지한 채
사방을 살펴보니

말미잘이 반갑다고
손짓하고
물고기가 친구 하자며
가까이 왔다가
사라진다

때로는
동족으로 보이는 듯

꽤 큰 물고기가
반갑다고
내 몸에 부딪혀
스쳐 지나간다.

Underwater Exploration

In the open sea
On deck
A dark sea
Jump into the middle

Relying on the lifeline
I looked everywhere

I'm glad to meet a sea anemone
Beckon
The fish are friends
Come close
Vanish

At times
Looks like a fellow

A pretty big fish
Nice to meet you
Hit my body
It passes by.

사바주 청사

둥근 원통형으로
지어진 로켓 빌딩

사바주의 미래를 상징하는
주 청사와 별관

사바주에서 가장 높은
건물로
세계 3대 건축물

기울어진 듯
사바주 청사가
소문이 나
관광자원이 되고 있다.

오늘도
관광객은
기울어진 주 청사를
지탱하는 포즈로
사진을 찍고 있다.

Sabah State Office

Round-cylindrical shape
Built rocket building

Symbolizing the future of Sabah
The main office and annex

The highest in Sabah
To the building
Three major buildings in the world

As if inclined
Sabah State Government House
A rumored
It is becoming a tourist resource

Today
Tourists
The leaning tower of Sabah
Supporting pose
They are taking a picture.

호수에 뜬 수상 가옥

연못보다 큰 호수
외나무다리로 연결된 판잣집
도시 속에 자리 잡고 있어
잘 보이지 않는다

그 호수엔
물이 별로 없다
물고기가 살지 않는다
식물도 잘 자라지 않는다

호수 주변에서 노는 아이들
표정이 밝다

과자를 나누어 줄 때는
어디서 왔는지
순식간에 모여든다

외국에서 탈출해온 주민으로
세월이 지나면 잘되리라는 듯
희망의 눈빛을 보인다.

A House Built Over The Lake

A lake larger than a pond
The shack connected to a wooden bridge
It's in the city
Be invisible

In that lake
Be very waterless
Fish do not live
Plants don't grow well either

Children playing around the lake
Have a bright face

When you distribute the cookies
Where you're from
Come together in a flash

A resident who has escaped from a foreign country
As if it would work out over time
They look hopeful.

갠지스강 블루스

초판인쇄 2021년 7월 10일 초판발행 2021년 7월 15일

지은이 장현경
펴낸이 장현경 펴낸곳 엘리트출판사
등록일 2013년 2월 22일 제2013-10호

서울특별시 광진구 긴고랑로15길 11 (중곡동)
전화 010-5338-7925
E-mail : wedgus@hanmail.net

정가 12,000원

ISBN 979-11-87573-29-6 03810